JABBERWOCKY

Lewis Carroll's
JABBERWOCKY

Illustrations by Jane Breskin Zalben

With Annotations by Humpty Dumpty

CAROLINE HOUSE

Illustrations copyright © 1977 by Jane Breskin Zalben
All rights reserved • Published by Caroline House
Boyds Mills Press, Inc. • A Highlights Company
910 Church Street • Honesdale, Pennsylvania 18431
Originally published by Frederick Warne and Co., Inc., New York, 1977

Publisher Cataloging-in-Publication Data
Carroll, Lewis, 1832-1898.
Lewis Carroll's Jabberwocky/illustrations by Jane Breskin Zalben.
Originally published by Frederick Warne and Co., Inc., New York, 1977.
[32] p.: col. ill. ; cm.
Summary: A finely illustrated classic nonsense poem taken from
Through the Looking Glass, and what Alice found there.
1. Children's poetry, English. 2. Nonsense verse, English. (1. Nonsense verse.)
I. Zalben, Jane Breskin, ill. II. Title. 821/.8—dc20
Library of Congress Catalog Card Number: 91-76066 • ISBN 1-56397-080-5

Book designed by Jane Breskin Zalben
Distributed by St. Martin's Press
Printed in Hong Kong

To my good friends
on all your 364 un-birthdays
and the feelings you give me

There was a book lying near Alice on the table, and while she sat watching the White King (for she was still a little anxious about him, and had the ink all ready to throw over him, in case he fainted again), she turned over the leaves, to find some part that she could read, "—for it's all in some language I don't know," she said to herself.

It was like this.

JABBERWOCKY

'Twas brillig, and the slithy toves
Did gyre and gimble in the wabe:
All mimsy were the borogoves,
And the mome raths outgrabe.

She puzzled over this for some time, but at last a bright thought struck her. "Why, it's a Looking-glass book, of course! And, if I hold it up to a glass, the words will all go the right way again."

This was the poem that Alice read:

Twas brillig, and the slithy toves
Did gyre and gimble in the wabe:

All mimsy were the borogoves,

And the mome raths outgrabe.

"Beware the Jabberwock, my son!
The jaws that bite, the claws that catch!

Beware the Jubjub bird, and shun
The frumious Bandersnatch!"

He took his vorpal sword in hand:
    Long time the manxome foe he sought—

So rested he by the Tumtum tree,
And stood awhile in thought.

And, as in uffish thought he stood,
    The Jabberwock, with eyes of flame,
Came whiffling through the tulgey wood,
    And burbled as it came!

One, two! One, two! And through and through
The vorpal blade went snicker-snack!

He left it dead, and with its head
He went galumphing back.

"And hast thou slain the Jabberwock?
    Come to my arms, my beamish boy!
O frabjous day! Callooh! Callay!"
    He chortled in his joy.

'Twas brillig, and the slithy toves
    Did gyre and gimble in the wabe:
All mimsy were the borogoves,
    And the mome raths outgrabe.

ANNOTATIONS BY HUMPTY DUMPTY

"You seem very clever at explaining words, Sir," said Alice. "Would you kindly tell me the meaning of the poem called 'Jabberwocky'?"

"Let's hear it," said Humpty Dumpty. "I can explain all the poems that ever were invented—and a good many that haven't been invented just yet."

This sounded very hopeful, so Alice repeated the first verse:—

> " 'Twas brillig, and the slithy toves
>   Did gyre and gimble in the wabe:
> All mimsy were the borogoves,
>   And the mome raths outgrabe."

"That's enough to begin with," Humpty Dumpty interrupted: "there are plenty of hard words there. 'Brillig' means four o'clock in the afternoon—the time when you begin broiling things for dinner."

"That'll do very well," said Alice: "and '*slithy*'?"

"Well, '*slithy*' means 'lithe and slimy.' 'Lithe' is the same as 'active.' You see it's like a portmanteau—there are two meanings packed up into one word."

"I see it now," Alice remarked thoughtfully: "and what are '*toves*'?"

"Well, '*toves*' are something like badgers—they're something like lizards—and they're something like corkscrews."

"They must be very curious-looking creatures."

"They are that," said Humpty Dumpty: "also they make their nests under sundials — also they live on cheese."

"And what's to '*gyre*' and to '*gimble*'?"

"To '*gyre*' is to go round and round like a gyroscope. To '*gimble*' is to make holes like a gimlet."

"And '*the wabe*' is the grass-plot round a sundial, I suppose?" said Alice, surprised at her own ingenuity.

"Of course it is. It's called '*wabe*' you know, because it goes a long way before it, and a long way behind it—"

"And a long way beyond it on each side," Alice added.

"Exactly so. Well then, *'mimsy'* is 'flimsy and miserable' (there's another portmanteau for you). And a *'borogove'* is a thin shabby-looking bird with its feathers sticking out all round—something like a live mop."

"And then *'mome raths'*?" said Alice. "I'm afraid I'm giving you a great deal of trouble."

"Well, a *'rath'* is a sort of green pig: but *'mome'* I'm not certain about. I think it's short for 'from home'—meaning that they'd lost their way, you know."

"And what does *'outgrabe'* mean?"

"Well, *'outgribing'* is something between bellowing and whistling, with a kind of sneeze in the middle: however, you'll hear it done, maybe —down in the wood yonder—and, when you've once heard it, you'll be *quite* content. Who's been repeating all that hard stuff to you?"

"I read it in a book" said Alice.

JABBERWOCKY

'Twas brillig, and the slithy toves
    Did gyre and gimble in the wabe:
All mimsy were the borogoves,
    And the mome raths outgrabe.

"Beware the Jabberwock, my son!
    The jaws that bite, the claws that catch!
Beware the Jubjub bird, and shun
    The frumious Bandersnatch!"

He took his vorpal sword in hand:
    Long time the manxome foe he sought—
So rested he by the Tumtum tree,
    And stood awhile in thought.

And, as in uffish thought he stood,
    The Jabberwock, with eyes of flame,
Came whiffling through the tulgey wood,
    And burbled as it came!

One, two! One, two! And through and through
    The vorpal blade went snicker-snack!
He left it dead, and with its head
    He went galumphing back.

"And hast thou slain the Jabberwock?
    Come to my arms, my beamish boy!
O frabjous day! Callooh! Callay!"
    He chortled in his joy.

'Twas brillig, and the slithy toves
    Did gyre and gimble in the wabe:
All mimsy were the borogoves,
    And the mome raths outgrabe.

The full color art was done with 000 brush
on Opaline Parchment with watercolors.
The display and text type was set in
Egmont Light at the Royal Composing Room.
The book was color separated by Dichroic Color Inc.
Typography by Jane Breskin Zalben